I'm Going To READ!

These levels are meant only as guides;
you and your child can best choose a book that's right.

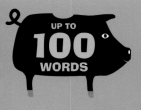

Level 1: Kindergarten–Grade 1 . . . Ages 4–6

UP TO 50 WORDS

- word bank to highlight new words
- consistent placement of text to promote readability
- easy words and phrases
- simple sentences build to make simple stories
- art and design help new readers decode text

Level 2: Grade 1 . . . Ages 6–7

UP TO 100 WORDS

- word bank to highlight new words
- rhyming texts introduced
- more difficult words, but vocabulary is still limited
- longer sentences and longer stories
- designed for easy readability

Level 3: Grade 2 . . . Ages 7–8

UP TO 200 WORDS

- richer vocabulary of up to 200 different words
- varied sentence structure
- high-interest stories with longer plots
- designed to promote independent reading

Level 4: Grades 3 and up . . . Ages 8 and up

MORE THAN 300 WORDS

- richer vocabulary of more than 300 different words
- short chapters, multiple stories, or poems
- more complex plots for the newly independent reader
- emphasis on reading for meaning

LEVEL 2

2 4 6 8 10 9 7 5 3 1

Published by Sterling Publishing Co., Inc.
387 Park Avenue South, New York, NY 10016
Text copyright © 2006 by Harriet Ziefert Inc.
Illustrations copyright © 2006 by Yukiko Kido
Distributed in Canada by Sterling Publishing
c/o Canadian Manda Group, 165 Dufferin Street
Toronto, Ontario, Canada M6K 3H6
Distributed in Great Britain and Europe by Chris Lloyd at Orca Book
Services, Stanley House, Fleets Lane, Poole BH15 3AJ, England
Distributed in Australia by Capricorn Link (Australia) Pty. Ltd.
P.O. Box 704, Windsor, NSW 2756, Australia

I'm Going To Read is a trademark of Sterling Publishing Co., Inc.

Library of Congress Cataloging-in-Publication Data

Kido, Yukiko.
Who's at the movies / pictures by Yukiko Kido.
    p. cm. — (I'm going to read)
Summary: Nomi and her friends get a surprise when they go
to see a science fiction movie.
ISBN 1-4027-3340-2
[1. Motion pictures—Fiction. 2. Extraterrestrial beings—Fiction.]
I. Title. II. Series.

PZ7.K5334Nom 2006
[E]—dc22   2005018752

Printed in China
All rights reserved

Sterling ISBN 13: 978-1-4027-3340-6
Sterling ISBN 10: 1-4027-3340-2

For information about custom editions, special sales, premium and
corporate purchases, please contact Sterling Special Sales
Department at 800-805-5489 or specialsales@sterlingpub.com.

Who's
at the
Movies?

Pictures by Yukiko Kido

Sterling Publishing Co., Inc.
New York

This is Nomi.

Nomi's friends
are Ken and Kira.

"Let's go to the movies,"
says Nomi.

line   long   tickets

Nomi, Ken, and Kira
wait in a long line to buy tickets.

Ken buys
candy.

Kira buys popcorn.
"Extra butter, please!"
she says.

Nomi finds an empty row.

"Let's sit here,"
she says.

Soon the lights
are turned off.

Visitor From A Distant Planet

It is dark. Very dark.
The movie begins.

The green alien is large.
Very large.

Nomi turns around
and points.

"Look, Kira,"
she says.

"Shhh!" says Ken.
"Be quiet and watch!"

be   watch

"No talking at the movies,"
says Ken.
"Just be quiet."

"But I see something
strange . . . very strange,"
says Nomi.

"Follow me!"
says Nomi.